friends?

Dee Phillips

RiGHT NOW!

Blast

Dare

Dumped

Eject

Fight

Friends?

Goal

Goodbye

Grind

Joyride

Mirror

Scout

First published by Evans Brothers Limited

2A Portman Mansions, Chiltern Street, London W1U 6NR, United Kingdom

Copyright © Ruby Tuesday Books Limited 2010

This edition published under license from Evans Limited

SADDLEBACK
EDUCATIONAL PUBLISHING
www.sdlback.com

ISBN-13: 978-1-62250-882-2
ISBN-10: 1-62250-882-3
eBook: 978-1-63078-017-3

Printed in Malaysia

20 19 18 17 16   2 3 4 5 6

That night I went online.
There was a message.
Join the group:
Sam Clark is so fat she killed her horse.

friends?

The room is very hot.
We are all waiting.
I look at Mom.
She says, "It will be OK, Gaby."

But I don't know.

I wish I could turn
back time.

It started one Saturday morning.
I was online with my friends.

Gaby:

What are we doing today?

Alisha:

I want to go to the mall.

Dylan might be there.

Kelly:

Not Dylan again!!!!!

Ella:

You are SO sad Alisha.

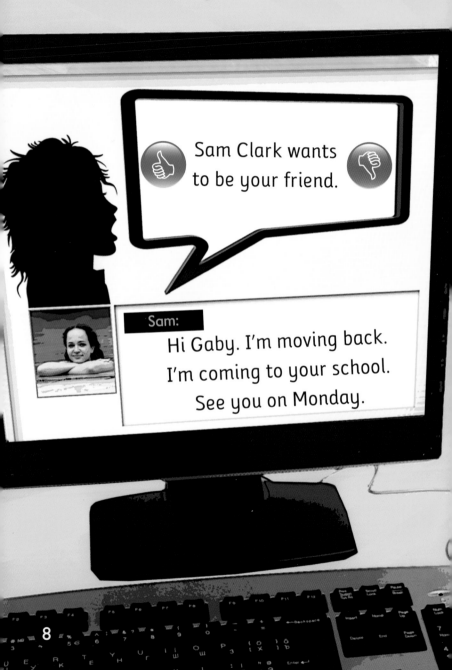

I add Sam to my friends list.

Sam was my friend a long time ago.
Then her dad got rich.
Her family moved away.
Sam went to a private school.

Sam was in my class on Monday.
She looked sad.

She said, "Dad lost all our money.
We had to sell our house."

11

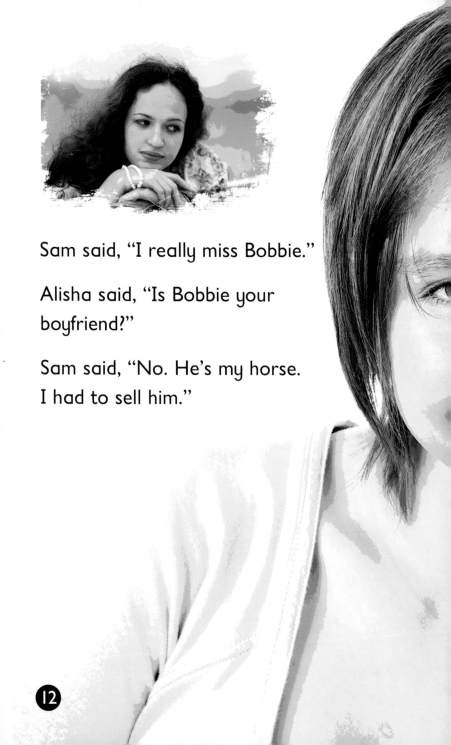

Sam said, "I really miss Bobbie."

Alisha said, "Is Bobbie your boyfriend?"

Sam said, "No. He's my horse. I had to sell him."

I saw Alisha give Ella a look.

I felt sorry for Sam.

That afternoon it was basketball.
I picked the team. Alisha. Kelly. Ella.
Alisha said, "Pick Carly. She's good."

But Sam was standing alone.
I picked Sam.
Alisha said, "No way!"

We lost the game.

Alisha was angry.

Sam said, "Sorry. I'm bad at sports."

Alisha said, "You should stick to horses."

Then she walked away with Ella.

That night Alisha was still angry.

Alisha:
My Little Pony totally lost us the game.

Ella:
My Little Pony. LOL.

Gaby:
Just leave it A.

Alisha:
Whose side are you on Gaby?

I logged off.

Alisha would get bored with this.
She always did.

Sam wasn't at school on Tuesday.
Or Wednesday.

Alisha:

Where's My Little Pony?

Kelly:

Maybe she's gone back to her old snobby school.

On Thursday there was a message.

Sam:

I've been really upset.
Bobbie's new owner called me.
Bobbie broke his leg and
had to be shot.
RIP. Bobbie.

Sam came to school on Friday.
But she kept crying.

Alisha said, "God. It was only a horse."

Sam got really upset. She shouted, "You're so stupid. You don't know anything!"

Alisha was really angry.

Friday night we were online.

Alisha:

My Little Pony is SO stuck up.

Gaby:

Don't be mean Alisha.

Alisha:
She smells like a horse!

Kelly:
LOL

Ella:
You are SO bad Alisha.

Alisha:
MLP is so fat.
No wonder her horse's leg broke!

27

Saturday night was the same.

I logged off.
Alisha would get bored soon.
She always did.

Alisha:

Did you see MLP in McDonald's?

Kelly:

I thought I could smell a horse.

Alisha:

Maybe Bobbie is a burger now.

Ella:

Yuck! You are sick Alisha.

Sam:

Leave me alone.
What have I done to you?

On Sunday I went online.

Alisha:

MLP is a stuck up cow.

Kelly:

Boohoo. Leave me alone.

Ella:

What have I done to you?
Boohoo.

Alisha:

God I hate her.

On Monday Sam wasn't at school.

That night I went online.
There was a message.

Join the group:

Sam Clark is so fat
she killed her horse.

On Tuesday night I went online.
There was just one message.

Sam:

STOP. Please.

Then Mrs. Clark called Mom.

That's why we're here.
Mom and I.
Mr. and Mrs. Clark.

Mrs. Clark says, "Thanks for coming,
Gaby. You are a good friend."

But I'm not so sure.

Sam took lots of painkillers.
The doctors are trying to wake her up.

So now we are all just waiting.
Waiting in this hot room.

A doctor comes in.
I look down at my phone.
Mr. and Mrs. Clark stand up.

I look at the doctor's face.

I press Send.

Gaby:

I'm sorry.
Your friend.

SAFER NETWORKING
ON YOUR OWN

Social networking sites can be great fun, but if they are abused, they can cause a lot of unhappiness.

• Make up a name for a new social networking site.

• List some special features of the new site. Try to think of things that no other sites have!

• Write a "behavior code" for people using your site. What other things could be done to make networking safer?

WHAT WOULD YOU DO?
WITH A PARTNER

The story is about a girl being bullied online. However, Sam was sad even before she got to Gaby's school.

• Look back through the book. Think of as many different reasons as you can to explain why Sam took the pills.

• What would you have done if you had been one of the friends?

Join the group:

Sam Clark is so fat she killed her horse.

44

WHO'S TO BLAME?
IN A GROUP

Discuss with your group who is to blame for what happened:

- Alisha, because she leads the bullying?
- Ella or Kelly, for encouraging Alisha?
- Gaby, for standing by and letting it happen?
- Sam, for letting the bullying get to her?
- Or perhaps the Internet is to blame?

HOW DOES IT END?
ON YOUR OWN / WITH A PARTNER / IN A GROUP

Does Sam live? Or does she die? Decide how the story ends, and then imagine the next day.

- If you are working with a partner or in a group, role-play two or more of the characters meeting at the mall.

- If you are working on your own, create a computer screen that shows an online chat between the friends. How does each girl react to the news?

IF YOU ENJOYED
THIS BOOK,
TRY THESE OTHER
RIGHT NOW!
BOOKS.

Will hates what he sees in the mirror. Brenna does too. Their lives would be so much better if they looked different.

Eric's fighter jet is under attack. There's only one way to escape ...

Laci and Jaden were in love, but now it's over. So why is Jaden always watching her?

FIGHT

It's Saturday night.
Two angry guys. Two knives.
There's going to be a fight.

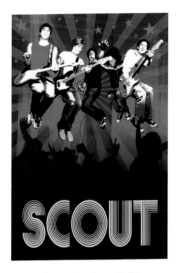

SCOUT

Tonight is the band's big
chance. Tonight, a record
company scout is at their gig!

BLAST

Damien's platoon is under
attack. Another soldier is in
danger. Damien must risk his
own life to save him.

DARE

It's just an old, empty house.
Kristi must spend the night
inside. Just Kristi and
the ghost ...

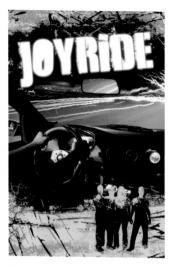

Tanner sees the red car. The keys are inside. Tanner says to Jacob, Bailey, and Hannah, "Want to go for a drive?"

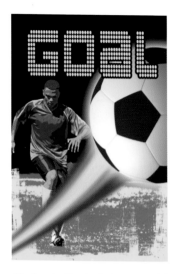

Today is Carlos's tryout with Chivas. There's just one place up for grabs. But today, everything is going wrong!

Taylor hates this new town. She misses her friends. There's nowhere to skate!

Tonight, Kayla must make a choice. Stay in Philadelphia with her boyfriend, Ryan. Or start a new life in California.